MORAG HOOD

I AM BAT

TWO HOOTS

I AM BAT.

I do not like mornings.

I like **CHERRIES**.

They are my

FAVOURITE

of all things.

They are

JUICY

and

RED

and

DELICIOUS

and . . .

...THEY ARE MINE.

Do **NOT**

take my cherries.

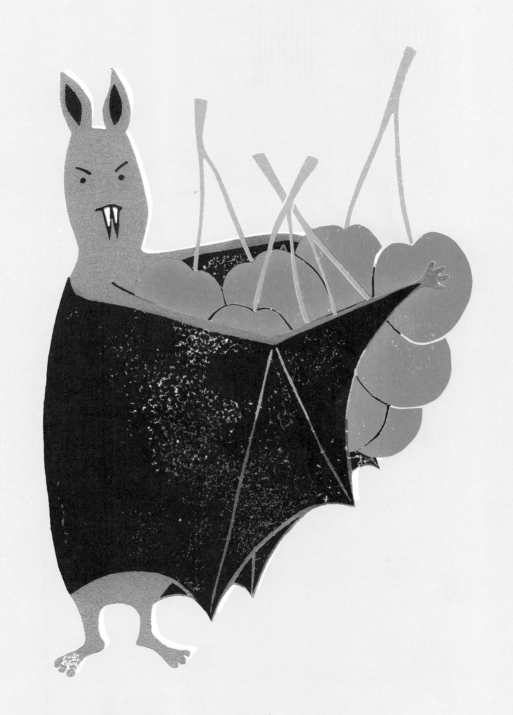

If you take my

cherries

I will be

ANGRY.

I will be **FEROCIOUS** like a lion.

(But smaller and with wings.)

I will just
leave my
cherries
here.
DO
NOT
touch
them.

I WILL KNOW IF
YOU TAKE ONE.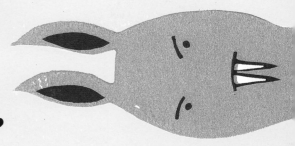

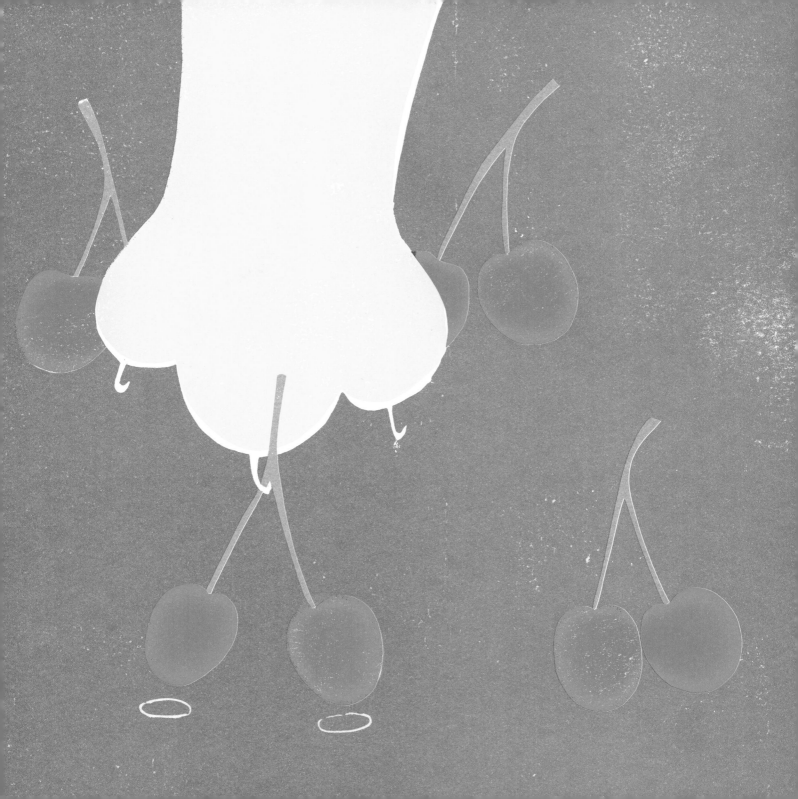

My
CHERRIES!
Some of them are
MISSING.

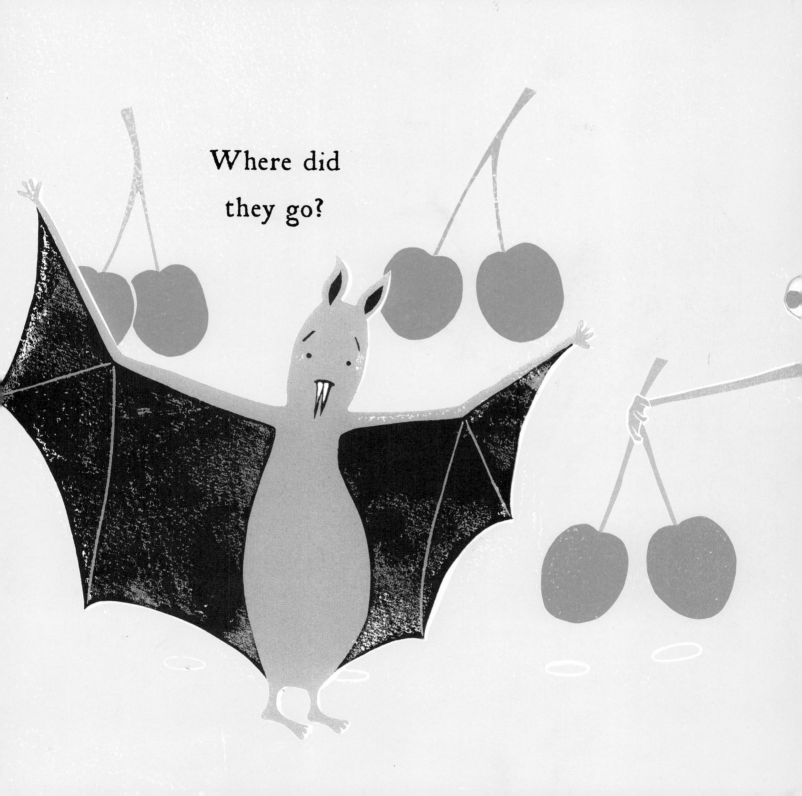

Who stole my **CHERRIES?**

Was it

YOU?

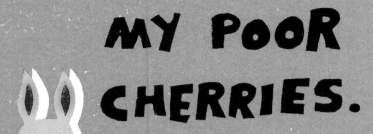

MY POOR
CHERRIES.

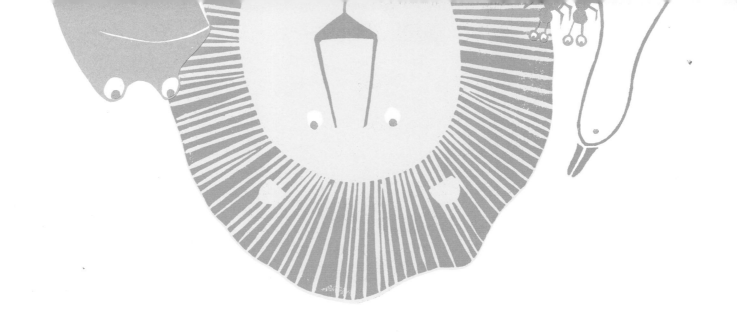

I will **NEVER** be happy again.

Ooh . . .

A PEAR!

I like **PEARS.**

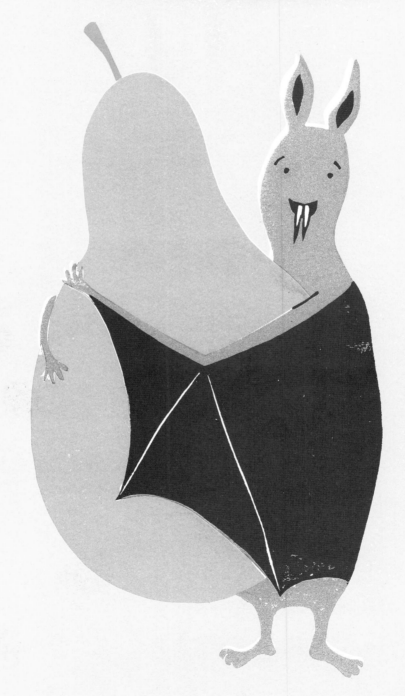

I AM
BAT.

DO
NOT
TAKE
MY
PEAR.